Miss B is a hugely motivated individual with a massive zest for life who began writing for personal enjoyment shortly after giving birth to her daughter. Her journey with mindfulness began at this time and this inspired her to write her debut publication; *Be Positive with Lola*. She hopes to show children from a very young age that with positive thinking and kindness, comes happiness. Mel spends her days providing office support for a car performance garage, teaches fitness classes, writes when she can and best of all, spends time with her loved ones. She describes herself as "a busy Mum who loves life and the people she's lucky enough to share it with."

AUSTIN MACAULEY PUBLISHERS™

LONDON • CAMBRIDGE • NEW YORK • SHARJAH

BE POSITIVE

with

Lola

Miss B

A CIP catalogue record for this title is available from the British Library.

ISBN 9781528993203 (Paperback)
ISBN 9781528993210 (ePub e-book)

www.austinmacauley.com

First Published (2020)
Austin Macauley Publishers Ltd
25 Canada Square
Canary Wharf
London
E14 5LQ

To my darling daughter, Bella – I may have given you life but you gave me my life back. Love you always.

Lola woke with a really big grin.
She jumped out of bed and started to sing,
"Good morning, Mummy. Good morning, everyone.
Today's going to be a great day – just look at that sun!"

The sky was blue, there wasn't a cloud in sight.
She thought the beauty in nature was an absolute delight.
She looked to the distance and got ready to say
the little phrase her mum taught her to focus on each day:

I am special, I am loved and I am bright.
Be kind, smile big and be polite.
Lola smiled and took a deep breath in.
She looked out of the window and repeated it again:
I am special, I am loved and I am bright.
Be kind, smile big and be polite.

This was a kind of mantra Lola repeated, come what may,
especially in times she felt upset or rarely led astray.
It helped her to remain in the moment and take a big sigh of relief.
The only difference between a smile and a frown is a positive belief.

She dressed herself in her uniform and got her bags ready.
She was dancing around the room when her mum yelled,
"Lola, please go steady!"

"But Mum, I can't. I'm too excited.
It's the first day of term and I'll get reunited
with all the books and the fun things to learn,
and of course, my best friend: her name is Fern."

Down for breakfast,
A quick piece of toast
and of course, a piece of fruit
she enjoyed that the most.

"Bye Mummy. I'm off to school now,"
she waved to her mum, and the cat
said *"meeeow"*.
Her mum shouted, "I love you" as she
walked out of the door.
Lola shouted through the letterbox,
"Mum, I love you more!!!"

With a positive mind and a spring in her step,
she walked to school; she skipped and she leapt.
She waved to passers-by and received smiles back,
she even managed a giggle – see if you can do that!

She noticed so much as she looked up and down.
The trees blew in the wind as the leaves were turning brown.
Flowers still bloomed and were colours of all kind.
Birds sang away as they searched to see what they could find.

Ding, ding, ding! There goes the bell.
She hurried to class although she knew very well
that despite her intelligence, despite her smile,
there would sometimes be that one nasty child.

Sure enough, as the class begun,
Billy saw Lola and stuck out his tongue.
Then came the words, "Lola, Lola with the big mole!"
The other boys laughed. I think that was his goal.

Lola still smiled, helped others and kept strong.
She knew the bullies would one day realise they were wrong,
for the true beauty in life is making people feel happy,
there's no self-satisfaction from making others feel crappy.

The first lesson was science: the lesson of wonder.
Today, they looked into the beauty of thunder.
A noise that occurs after a bolt of lightning.
Lola found it fascinating whilst others said it was frightening.

Next was maths and not the simple kind.
They were learning to see what patterns they could find.
4, 10, 22, what number followed next?
Some of the class loved the challenge and others liked it less.

Fern met her at play time as they were in a different class.
This part of the day always whizzed-by so very fast.
Hop scotch was played first, followed by a walk
When they got together – blimey – they could talk.

They told each other everything, even when it made them sad.
Confiding in someone you trust means a problem never seems so bad.
Lola knew she did not have lots of friends, but she did not mind that.
She had the very best one around and that was a fact.

The last lesson of the day was Drama and Expressive Arts.
Billy was on form and started tearing Lola apart.
She wondered what she had ever done to make him want to be mean.
Would he be sorry one day? That was yet to be seen.

Lola, in the moment, quickly closed her eyes,
If she said she was not hurt at all, she would be telling us lies.
I am special, I am loved and I am bright.
Be kind, smile big and be polite.
(and Breeeethe)

Some people hide their true feelings by acting a different way.
You see, Billy actually liked Lola the best, but he could never say.
Billy was taught to hide his feelings and be tough.
Little did he know that this had made them both feel rough.

As the lesson continued, Lola beamed and had so much fun.
She loved singing and dancing; she was always the enthusiastic one.
They watched a play and they studied it too.
Did you know that Shakespeare went to heaven when he was only 52?

Ding, ding, ding, another bell.
"Home time, children," the teacher yelled.
See you all tomorrow when we will elaborate on today.
Please make sure you do our homework, no excuse will be okay.

On the little walk home, Lola listened to her tunes.
She looked into the sky and saw some beautiful balloons.
As they floated away so careless and free,
Lola thought to herself how pretty something so simple can be.

"How was school, darling?" her mum asked away,
"I was bullied a little, Mummy, but I am okay.
I remember what you taught me: to always be kind,
even to those you feel are not worth your time.
For you never know what they may face;
the world can be a very scary place.

Besides that, it really was a lovely day.
We learnt about Shakespeare and got to watch a play."
Lola continued to tell her about a day full of fun,
Then she said, "Didn't I tell you it would be a good day
when I woke, Mum?"

Believe. Achieve. Love. Smile.